Flower Fairies of the Spring
~A~
Celebration

◆

Flower Fairies of the Spring

~ A ~ Celebration

◆

CICELY MARY BARKER

FREDERICK WARNE

The reproductions in this book have been made using the most modern electronic scanning methods
from entirely new transparencies of Cicely Mary Barker's original watercolours.
They enable Cicely Mary Barker's skill as an artist to be appreciated as never before.

FREDERICK WARNE

Published by the Penguin Group
27 Wrights Lane, London W8 5TZ, England
Penguin Putnam Inc., 375 Hudson Street, New York, New York 10014, USA
Penguin Books Australia Ltd, Ringwood, Victoria, Australia
Penguin Books Canada Ltd, 10 Alcorn Avenue, Toronto, Ontario, Canada M4V 3B2
Penguin Books (NZ) Ltd, 182-190 Wairau Road, Auckland 10, New Zealand

Penguin Books Ltd, Registered Offices: Harmondsworth, Middlesex, England

First published in 1998

ISBN 0 7232 4433 2

Colour reproduction by Saxon Photolitho Ltd, Norwich
Printed and bound in Singapore by Imago Publishing Ltd.

ILLUSTRATION ACKNOWLEDGEMENTS
The publishers would like to thank the following for their kind permission to reproduce
the photographs and illustrations which appear on the pages listed below.
Annie Poole, A-Z Botanical Collection Ltd., 26
Joan Dear, The Garden Picture Library, 28
W. Broadhurst, A-Z Botanical Collection Ltd., 30
Courtesy of Martin Barker: 9, 12, 15, 17, 25, 26, 28, 30
Courtesy of Geoffrey Oswald: 14, 24

~ Contents ~

~ Spring Magic ~

The World is very old;
    But year by year
It groweth new again
    When buds appear.

The World is very old,
    And sometimes sad;
But when the daisies come
    The World is glad.

The World is very old;
    But every Spring
It groweth young again,
    And fairies sing.

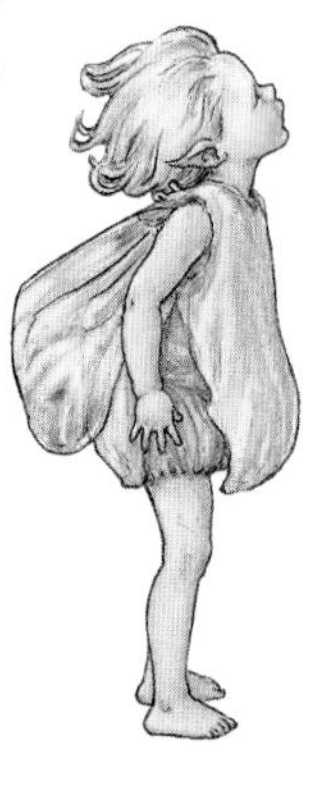

~ Cicely Mary Barker ~

Cicely Mary Barker lived most of her life in Croydon, South London, but her imagination and artistry enabled her to envisage an invisible world that extended far beyond suburban Surrey. This magical realm, populated by fairies, was captured in her delightful poems and delicate drawings. Though she lived a quiet, modest life, Cicely Mary Barker achieved commercial success and world-wide renown with her Flower Fairies books. Today the public remains as enchanted with her creations as it was 75 years ago, when *Flower Fairies of the Spring* was first published.

Born on 28th June 1895 in Croydon, Cicely Mary Barker was the second child of Mary and Walter Barker. A frail child who suffered from epilepsy, Cicely was sheltered from the outside world by her parents and her older sister, Dorothy. The Barkers were a comfortable middle class family and they employed a nanny to educate Cicely at home and a cook to prepare her special meals. Despite her ill-health, Cicely enjoyed a happy, secure childhood and entertained herself with books and drawing.

Cicely's talent, evident from an early age, flourished quickly with the encouragement of her family and friends. Walter Barker, a partner in a seed supply company, was a capable watercolourist and he nurtured his youngest daughter's talent for drawing. When the family went on holiday, Cicely and her devoted father would sketch together by the seaside. Cicely's father enrolled her in a correspondence course for art tuition in 1908. That same year, aged only 13 years old, Cicely exhibited her work at the Croydon Art Society. In 1911, Cicely's father sold four of her drawings to the printer Raphael Tuck. Cicely also won second prize in the Croydon Art Society poster design competition and was elected a life member of the society. At 16 years old, Cicely was well on the way to a highly successful career.

*Cicely Mary Barker
as a young woman*

Unfortunately, Walter Barker did not live long enough to witness his daughter's rise to fame. He died in 1912 from a virus at the age of 43. His family sought comfort in their Christian faith but faced tightened economic circumstances. Dorothy, the more serious and practical of the two sisters, assumed the role of breadwinner. Having trained as a teacher, she began to teach a kindergarten class. Dorothy's salary enabled Cicely to continue drawing and pursuing her artistic goals.

Cicely contributed to the household finances by selling her poems and artwork to magazines such as *Child's Own*, *My Magazine* and Raphael Tuck annuals. She won a competition in 1914 sponsored by *The Challenge* magazine for her 'portrait of the editor as I imagine him to be'. Her early commercial work also included several series of watercolour postcards. The patriotic themes of the *Shakespeare's Children* and *Picturesque Children of the Allies* series proved very popular during the First World War. A charming precursor of her later work, Cicely's set of six *Fairy Cards* was commissioned by the S. Harvey Fine Art Publishing Co.

Between 1917 and 1918, Cicely embarked on the project that was to be her most famous. The Flower Fairies illustrations beautifully merged two of her favourite subjects—children and nature. Influenced by the Pre-Raphaelite artists, Cicely adhered to their practice of painting directly from nature. Cicely made numerous sketches of flowers to ensure that her drawings were botanically accurate and used local children as models. Gladys Tidy, the girl who did the Barkers' P9 .60 housework, sat for the Primrose Fairy. Wearing costumes made by Cicely, the young models posed holding the flower they were representing. Cicely's paintings skilfully convey the children's personalities as well as the flowers' appearances.

It was not until 1923 that Cicely searched for a publisher for *Flower Fairies of the Spring*. Although she received several rejections, Blackie accepted the work and paid her £25 for the 24 poems and paintings. The book was an instant success. In the first edition copies of *Flower Fairies of the Spring* that she presented to her mother and sister, Cicely inscribed sentimental poems expressing her gratitude for their support. The poem dedicated to Dorothy not only demonstrates respect and affection, but also reveals Cicely's concern about the effects of industrialization on the countryside.

Cicely Mary Barker (left) with her mother and sister Dorothy

To DOB
By hedge and footpath, Hills and Hurst,
Ere modern change had wrought its worst,
Went you and I on Saturdays,
And learnt the flowers and their ways.
To you, best Teacher, do I owe
The seed from which these fairies grow;
Take then this Little Book the First
Sprung from old lanes and fields and Hurst.

An unworldly character, Cicely remained protected by her family from the outside world in adult life. It was her mother, for example, who wrote to Blackie before the publication of *Flower Fairies of the Summer* to ensure that Cicely received royalties for her work. As a result of being babied, Cicely retained a certain innocence and simplicity evident in her poetry.

The three Barker women moved to a smaller house in Croydon in 1924, where Dorothy established her own kindergarten and Cicely built a studio in the garden. Using her sister's pupils for inspiration and as models, Cicely continued her work on the Flower Fairies, producing a total of seven books for Blackie. Today, however, there are eight Flower Fairies titles in print. In 1985, Cicely's publishers compiled the volume *Flower Fairies of the Winter* from existing works, so there is now a book for every season.

The Flower Fairies were not Cicely's only work during the twenties, thirties and forties. Blackie commissioned her to illustrate the covers of their *New Nursery Series* story books. Cicely wrote and illustrated two classic tales of her own, *The Lord of the Rushie River* and *Groundsel and Necklaces*, and illustrated several collections of rhymes. In addition to her children's illustrations, Cicely painted many religious pictures during this period. Both Cicely and Dorothy Barker were Sunday school teachers and regular church-goers. A collaboration between the sisters produced a book of Bible stories entitled *He Leadeth Me*. Cicely also began painting church panels and altar pieces in 1929. Like the Pre-Raphaelite artists,

Cicely Mary Barker on holiday

Cicely used ordinary parishioners as models for her devotional works, such as *The Parable of the Great Supper* which hangs in St. George's Church, Waddon.

The Flower Fairies brought Cicely into contact with a fellow artist, Margaret Tarrant, who had painted her own versions of nature fairies. Though their styles were very different—Margaret's sprites were far more elfin and stylized than Cicely's naturalistic fairies—the two artists became close friends. They went on many sketching holidays together in Cornwall and along the South Coast. One of their favourite holiday destinations was Storrington in Sussex, where an artists' colony thrived.

Though Cicely was perhaps closer to her artist friends than to her sister, Dorothy was sadly missed when she died of a heart attack in 1954. After her sister's death, Cicely undertook responsibility for housekeeping and caring for her elderly mother. This left little time for painting and her commercial career came to a halt. The fifties were a sad decade for Cicely and saw the death of many close friends and her beloved aunt, Head Deaconess Alice Oswald. When her mother died in 1960, Cicely moved from Croydon to Sussex.

Cicely's friend Edith Major had passed away and left her a cottage near Storrington. The house proved impractical for an elderly woman, but Cicely leased a maisonette in Storrington which she named St. Andrews, after her local church in Croydon. Despite her failing eyesight and weakening body, Cicely remained the active vice-president of the Croydon Art Society between 1961 and 1972. On 16th February 1973, after several prolonged stays in nursing homes, Cicely died at the age of 77.

Cicely Mary Barker in later life

In her obituaries, Cicely Mary Barker was remembered for her kindness, sense of humour and Christian faith, as well as her prodigious artistic talent. Her ashes were scattered in a glade in Storrington churchyard, where she could remain close to the Sussex countryside that she so dearly loved. Cicely Mary Barker's spirit endures in her Flower Fairies, which still delight new generations of children and admirers 75 years after they first appeared.

~ A Fairy History ~

Fairies enjoyed a surge of popularity in the mid 19th century. Fanciful stories and fairy tales were deemed frivolous in the 18th century, but Victorian writers and artists embraced the genre as an artistic antidote to the Industrial Revolution. Whereas earlier children's literature existed only to educate, the Victorians wrote books to amuse children. A Liberal Member of Parliament, Edward H. Knatchbull-Hugessen wrote fairy tales as a pastime. In 1886, he defended the need for entertaining children's literature in *Friends and Foes from Fairy Land*:

> To my mind there is enough of dry, prosy matter stuffed into their poor brains in these dull times, and a little lighter food is as useful as it is welcome to them.

Eminent writers such as John Ruskin used fairy tales to describe an idyllic world, far removed from repressive, utilitarian society. Publishers such as Raphael Tuck made fairy tales an affordable mass-market commodity. Born at the end of a century that is often called the golden age of children's literature, Cicely Mary Barker owned books by Kate Greenaway and Randolph Caldecott as a child and her artwork recalls certain elements of their illustrations.

*Cicely Mary Barker's
childhood books*

The passion for pixies continued into the early 20th century. In the years prior to the First World War, technology developed at a rapid pace. Electricity precipitated the invention of the wireless, the telephone and the gramophone. This period also witnessed the spread of motor cars and the introduction of aeroplanes. Anxiety about the damaging

In 'Picturesque Children of the Allies', Cicely painted children wearing traditional costumes against their nation's flag. These cards, published in 1915, appealed to nationalist sentiment.

effects of these innovations was prevalent. Fairies, usually depicted in natural settings, represented a utopian alternative to modern life. Cicely, writing to a friend in 1923 after *Flower Fairies of the Spring* was published, lamented the disappearance of the countryside due to industrialization:

> There is no Cold Harbour Lane now, factories along Beddington Road; houses at the top of Russell Hill, and a Relief Road across it; fields chopped up; little streams drained away.

The success of the early Flower Fairies books, published after the destruction and carnage of the First World War, reveals the public's deep need for escapism through fancy. Similarly, the later Flower Fairies titles served to counter feelings of World War II gloom and malaise in the forties.

Cicely made frequent sketching trips to Sussex in the early forties to escape the damage of heavily bombed Croydon.

17

London hosted numerous avant garde exhibitions during the early 20th century, but Cicely was not influenced by the Cubist, Futurist or Surrealist movements of her day. Cicely's choice of subject may have been in vogue, but her style harks back to the Pre-Raphaelite artists who painted in the mid 19th century. These artists, led by Dante Gabriel Rossetti, William Holman Hunt and John Everett Millais, rejected chiaroscuro and art since the time of Raphael. Painting vibrant colours on white backgrounds, the Pre-Raphaelites called for 'truth to nature'. In 1899, the Barker family acquired a copy of *The Life and Letters of Sir John Everett Millais*. Cicely also admired Edward Burne-Jones and received the *Memorials of Edward Burne-Jones* as a Christmas present in 1920. Although some reviewers deemed her work outmoded, Cicely's Flower Fairies have stood the test of time and will continue to bring pleasure well into the 21st century.

A first edition cover printed in 1923

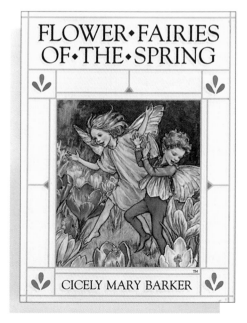

A recent cover, first printed in 1990

Throughout history, fairies have enjoyed popularity in times of economic depression or political strife. When humanity is at its emotional lowest, people look to the unknown to discover joy and magic. In the twenties, British illustrators such as Cicely, Margaret Tarrant and Arthur Rackham painted whimsical pictures to brighten the spirits of their despairing post-war contemporaries. Though fairies eventually went out of fashion, they are currently experiencing a resurgence of popularity. The prominence of the New Age movement, emphasising nature and the Earth, has sparked a new interest in nature sprites, or fairies. Fairy shops, art exhibitions and films about fairies have all appeared in the nineties, a decade that also produced an economic recession. With the millennium approaching and society increasingly dominated by computers, fairies represent a return to innocence and nature. Having fascinated humans since the Middle Ages, the fairy world will always serve an important role in culture. They may be invisible, but fairies are here to stay.

A selection of modern Flower Fairies merchandise

~ A Fairy Time Line ~

1846 Hans Christian Andersen's *Wonderful Stories for Children* arrived in England.

1848 Pre-Raphaelite Brotherhood formed. Members included Dante Gabriel Rossetti, John Everett Millais, William Holman Hunt and later, Edward Burne-Jones.

1862 Christina Rossetti's *Goblin Market* published. This fairy poem was a favourite of Cicely's.

1864 Richard Dadd, the insane painter, finished his fairy masterpiece *The Fairy Feller's Master-Stroke* in Bedlam Hospital.

1865 Lewis Carroll's *Alice's Adventures in Wonderland* published.

1878 Kate Greenaway's *Under the Window* published.

1888 Oscar Wilde's *The Happy Prince* published.

1895 Cicely Mary Barker born in Croydon, South London.

1898 Edward Burne-Jones, Pre-Raphaelite artist, died.

1901 Queen Victoria died and Edward VII crowned king.

1904 *Peter Pan* opened at the Duke of York's theatre in London to popular acclaim.

1905 Motor buses introduced in London, one year before the London Underground opened. Taxis had appeared in London the previous year.

1906 J. M. Barrie's *Peter Pan in Kensington Gardens* published, illustrated by Arthur Rackham. Cicely was given a copy of the book in 1908.

1910 King Edward VII died and George V acceded the throne.
Rewards and Fairies, Rudyard Kipling's stories about Puck, published.

1911 Cicely Mary Barker sold four artworks to Raphael Tuck, printer of story books and annuals.

1914 Britain declared war on Germany, beginning World War I. New military inventions cause unprecedented destruction.

1915 *Princess Mary's Gift Book* published, featuring fairy poems by Alfred Noyes.

1916 Arthur Rackham illustrated *The Allies Fairy Book*.

1917 Elsie Wright, aged 17, and her cousin Frances Griffiths, aged 9, claimed to have photographed fairies in Cottingley, Yorkshire.

1918 Germany surrendered to the Allied forces on 11th November, ending four years of global conflict.

1922 Arthur Conan Doyle published *The Coming of the Fairies*. Margaret Tarrant painted *Do You Believe in Fairies?*

1923 *Flower Fairies of the Spring* published.

1925 *Flower Fairies of the Summer* published.

1926 *Flower Fairies of the Autumn* published.

1929 *Peter Pan* ended its West End run. Cicely wrote a poem to the actress who played Peter, expressing her sadness. Blackie published several rhyme collections illustrated by Cicely. The Wall Street Crash plunged the world into the Great Depression.

1933 *He Leadeth Me* published by Blackie. *Arthur Rackham's Fairy Book* published.

1934 *A Flower Fairy Alphabet* published.

1937 Walt Disney released *Snow White and the Seven Dwarfs*, an animated feature film version of the Grimm's fairy tale.

1938 *The Lord of the Rushie River* published by Blackie.

1939 Britain and France declared war on Germany, beginning World War II.

1940 *Flower Fairies of the Trees* published.

1944 *Flower Fairies of the Garden* published.

1945 Germany surrendered on 8th May, or VE Day. Japan surrendered to the Allies on 14th August, bringing World War II to an end.

1946 *Groundsel and Necklaces*, now called *The Fairy Necklaces*, published by Blackie.

1948 *Flower Fairies of the Wayside* published by Blackie.

1949 Disney released the animated film of the fairy tale *Cinderella*.
C. S. Lewis wrote *The Lion, the Witch and the Wardrobe*, the first of the *Chronicles of Narnia* fantasy stories.

1953 Disney released a technicolour, animated version of *Peter Pan*.

1961 Cicely moved to Storrington, Sussex.

1966 *The Fellowship of the Rings* published, the first book in *The Lord of the Rings* trilogy by J. R. R. Tolkien.

1973 Cicely Mary Barker died in Storrington, Sussex.

1985 *Flower Fairies of the Winter* published, featuring apposite fairies compiled from the seven existing Flower Fairies books.

1990 Frederick Warne acquired rights from Blackie and published new editions of the eight Flower Fairies books.

1991 *Hook*, a feature film retelling of *Peter Pan*, released by director Steven Spielberg.

1997 *Fairytale: A True Story*, a film based on the Cottingley case, released.

1998 *Flower Fairies of the Spring* celebrated the 75th anniversary of its first publication.

~ The Making of a Flower Fairy ~

Dorothy Barker is pictured here with children from the kindergarten that she ran. Cicely frequently used her sister's pupils as models for the Flower Fairies.

Like the Pre-Raphaelite artists whom she admired, Cicely Mary Barker painted directly from nature and paid scrupulous attention to detail. The next few pages trace the artistic progression from flower to Flower Fairy. Cicely filled at least one sketchbook a year for all of her working life, leaving behind a rich collection of botanical drawings that help reveal how she worked. Though Cicely's Flower Fairies look delightfully effortless and whimsical, they are actually the result of painstaking craftsmanship.

Many of Cicely's sketches, drawn on her countryside holidays, are very polished and closely resemble the final Flower Fairies paintings. Detailed preparatory sketches allowed Cicely to concentrate on her models when she returned to her studio. Cicely drew her fairies from child models, but sadly few records exist of the preliminary sketches. Using Dion Clayton Calthrop's *English Costume* as reference, Cicely designed costumes for her models. These costumes, featuring wings made from twigs and gauze, echoed the colour, texture and shape of the flowers.

Flower Fairies of the Winter was compiled from the existing seven books in 1985. To create eight books of equal length, some of Cicely Mary Barker's original Flower Fairies were omitted from the new editions for editorial reasons. The out-of-print Flower Fairies featured on the following six pages exemplify Cicely's technique and highlight the botanical accuracy that was her hallmark.

These sketches, drawn sometime between 1919 and 1922, show Cicely's adeptness at capturing children in motion.

~ Scentless Mayweed ~

The Flower

This daisy-like flower is so-called to distinguish it from related plants with a strong smell. Blossoming between June and October, Scentless Mayweed grows on coastal cliffs. It is very likely that Cicely sketched Scentless Mayweed on one of her many seaside holidays.

SCENTLESS
MAYWEED,
OR
FEVERFEW

The Sketch

Cicely first sketched the flower's shape in pencil and then enhanced the form with colour. This pencil and watercolour sketch of Scentless Mayweed is a typical example of Cicely's method. Because the flower has white petals, Cicely shaded the background grey to provide contrast and brushed the petals with light brown paint for depth. A few, quick lines capably convey the plant's spiky leaves.

The SCENTLESS MAYWEED Fairy

The Painting

The Scentless Mayweed Fairy was included in the 1948 edition of *Flower Fairies of the Wayside*. In her introduction to the book, Cicely urged her readers to notice, 'How pretty common things can be!' Against a background of spiny leaves and stems, the Scentless Mayweed Fairy dances in the foreground, a graceful reminder of wayside flowers' oft-overlooked beauty.

Active like most of the *Wayside* fairies, the Scentless Mayweed Fairy holds her flower petal skirt and skips daintily across the page. Fashioned from green, spear-like leaves, her bodice is topped with a collar made from Scentless Mayweed stems. A flower-head bonnet crowns the ensemble, and juxtaposes the delicate flower with its common surroundings.

~ *Convolvulus* ~

The Flower

Convolvulus, also called field bindweed, flowers between June and September. The plant's tenacity makes it a garden nuisance, despite its pretty, sweet-smelling flowers. Convolvulus can grow nearly anywhere—from gardens to waste grounds—stubbornly creeping over any obstacle in its path and climbing to heights of two metres.

The Sketch

This pencil sketch displays Cicely's care and skill in reproducing the complicated form of these funnel-shaped flowers. In this sketch from 1920, Cicely drew Convolvulus from various angles. She also sketched examples of buds, enabling her to depict an entire vine of Convolvulus in the final painting. By drawing the veiny leaves and the flowers' pistils in minute detail, Cicely achieved great delicacy in the final painting.

The Painting

Cicely Mary Barker painted the Convolvulus Fairy for the first edition of *Flower Fairies of the Summer*, published in 1925. This watercolour illustration is a fine example of Cicely's early Flower Fairies. The pink and white flowers tumble in a diagonal from the top right-hand corner, suggesting the plant's rapid spread. Cicely creates another diagonal, running from the fairy's hat to the blossom he is smelling, which directs the viewer's eye into the middle of the composition. Cicely's costume design cleverly suggests the flower's appearance with loose, ruffled sleeves and a belt made from a length of stem. The plant's trumpet-shaped flower makes a perfect cap for the Convolvulus Fairy. Down on his hands and knees, the boy's pose mimicks bindweed's crawl over the ground. Details such as the boy's dimpled elbow and the flower's stamens demonstrate Cicely's equal skill at painting children and botany.

~ *Cat's-Ear* ~

The Flower

Cat's-Ear resembles a dandelion, but has a taller stalk. Flourishing anywhere from meadows to dunes and roadsides, this attractive yellow weed flowers in clusters between June and September.

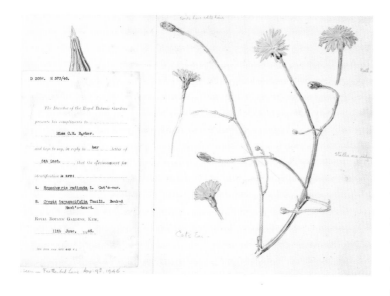

The Sketch

In the margins of her watercolour sketches, Cicely often wrote descriptive comments such as, 'buds have white hairs', to refresh her memory when she returned to her studio. When she could not identify a plant specimen, Cicely read *Wild Flowers as they Grow* by G. Clarke Nuttall or referred to the staff at Kew Gardens. As the letter attached to this sketch shows, Cicely sent samples of Cat's-Ear and Beaked Hawk's-Beard to the Royal Botanical Gardens in 1946 for identification. This sketch served as preparation for *Flower Fairies of the Wayside*, in which the Cat's-Ear fairy originally appeared.

The CAT'S-EAR Fairy

The Painting

The Cat's-Ear Fairy remains a pleasure to behold. Balancing on the stem with one arm reaching upwards, the fairy's extended pose reflects the plant's tall stalk. She wears a skirt made from an upside-down flower, with a shirt devised from the sepals. The Cat's-Ear Fairy grasps the entwined stems and camouflages herself behind the flowers. Eyes cast downwards, the Cat's-Ear Fairy smiles enigmatically and reminds the viewer of the elusive, hidden nature of the fairy world.

~ Spring Songs ~

Legend has it that fairies love music and dancing of all kinds, from lively reels to melancholy airs. Cicely Mary Barker's Flower Fairies are no exception and they made natural illustrations for sheet music. Cicely selected poems and pictures from *Flower Fairies of the Spring* and Olive Linnell set the verses to music. Their collaboration resulted in a music book entitled *Spring Songs with Music*, which was published by Blackie in 1924.

The Song of the Daisy Fairy

Very lightly and simply.

VOICE.

Come to me and play with me, I'm the ba-bies' flow - er; Make a neck-lace gay with me Spend the whole long day with me, Till the sun - set hour.

PIANO.

The book's popularity led to the publication of a further three music books in the twenties: *Summer Songs with Music*, *Autumn Songs with Music* and the compilation *Flower Songs of the Seasons*. In *Spring Songs*, Olive Linnell's music works harmoniously with the poems and pictures to bring the 12 Flower Fairies' personalities to life in a new medium. *The Song of the Daisy Fairy*, for example, is a suitably light and simple melody to accompany 'the babies' flower'. Although fairy melodies were once believed fatal to human ears, it is safe to assume that Linnell's sweet composition is harmless!

Flower Fairies of the Spring

The Crocus Fairies

~ The Song of ~
The Crocus Fairies

Crocus of yellow, new and gay;
Mauve and purple, in brave array;
  Crocus white
  Like a cup of light,—
Hundreds of them are smiling up,
Each with a flame in its shining cup,
By the touch of the warm and welcome sun
Opened suddenly. Spring's begun!
Dance then, fairies, for joy, and sing
The song of the coming again of Spring.

~ The Song of ~
The Snowdrop Fairy

The
Snowdrop
Fairy.

Deep sleeps the Winter,
Cold, wet, and grey;
Surely all the world is dead;
Spring is far away.
Wait! the world shall waken;
It is not dead, for lo,
The Fair Maids of February
Stand in the snow!

~ The Song of ~
The Colt's~Foot Fairy

The Colt's foot Fairy.

The winds of March are keen and cold;
I fear them not, for I am bold.

I wait not for my leaves to grow;
They follow after: they are slow.

My yellow blooms are brave and bright;
I greet the Spring with all my might.

~ The Song of ~
The Hazel~Catkin Fairy

Like little tails of little lambs,
  On leafless twigs my catkins swing;
They dingle-dangle merrily
  Before the wakening of Spring.

Beside the pollen-laden tails
  My tiny crimson tufts you see
The promise of the autumn nuts
  Upon the slender hazel tree.

While yet the woods lie grey and still
  I give my tidings: 'Spring is near!'
One day the land shall leap to life
  With fairies calling: 'Spring is HERE!'

The Hazel-Catkin Fairy.

The Hazel~Catkin Fairy

The Dead~Nettle Fairy

~ The Song of ~
The Dead-Nettle Fairy

Through sun and rain, and country lane,
The field, the road, are my abode.
Though leaf and bud be splashed with mud,
Who cares? Not I!—I see the sky,
The kindly sun, the wayside fun
Of tramping folk who smoke and joke,
The bairns who heed my dusty weed
(No sting have I to make them cry),
And truth to tell, they love me well.
My brothers, White, and Yellow bright,
Are finer chaps than I, perhaps;
Who cares? Not I! So now good-bye.

~ The Song of ~
The Willow~Catkin Fairy

The people call me Palm, they do;
They call me Pussy-willow too.
And when I'm full in bloom, the bees
Come humming round my yellow trees.

The people trample round about
And spoil the little trees, and shout;
My shiny twigs are thin and brown:
The people pull and break them down.

To keep a Holy Feast, they say,
They take my pretty boughs away.
I should be glad—I should not mind—
If only people weren't unkind.

Oh, you may pick a piece, you may
(So dear and silky, soft and grey);
But if you're rough and greedy, why
You'll make the little fairies cry.

(This catkin is the flower of the Sallow Willow.)

44

The
Willow-Catkin
Fairy.

The Willow~Catkin Fairy

~ THE SONG of ~
THE GROUNDSEL FAIRY

The Groundsel Fairy.

If dicky-birds should buy and sell
In tiny markets, I can tell
  The way they'd spend their money.
They'd ask the price of cherries sweet,
They'd choose the pinkest worms for meat,
And common Groundsel for a treat,
  Though *you* might think it funny.

Love me not, or love me well;
That's the way they'd buy and sell.

46

~ The Song of ~
The Stitchwort Fairy

The Stitchwort Fairy.

(A prettier name for Stitchwort is Starwort, but it is not so often used.)

I am brittle-stemmed and slender,
But the grass is my defender.

On the banks where grass is long,
I can stand erect and strong.

All my mass of starry faces
Looking up from wayside places,

From the thick and tangled grass,
Gives you greeting as you pass.

~ The Song of ~
The Windflower Fairy

While human-folk slumber,
    The fairies espy
Stars without number
    Sprinkling the sky.

The Winter's long sleeping,
    Like night-time, is done;
But day-stars are leaping
    To welcome the sun.

Star-like they sprinkle
    The wildwood with light;
Countless they twinkle—
    The Windflowers white!

('Windflower' is another name for Wood Anemone.)

48

The
Wind
-Flower
Fairy.

The Windflower Fairy

The Shepherd's-Purse Fairy.

The Shepherd's~Purse Fairy

~ The Song of ~
The Shepherd's ~ Purse Fairy

Though I'm poor to human eyes
Really I am rich and wise.
Every tiny flower I shed
Leaves a heart-shaped purse instead.

In each purse is wealth indeed—
Every coin a living seed.
Sow the seed upon the earth—
Living plants shall spring to birth.

Silly people's purses hold
Lifeless silver, clinking gold;
But you cannot grow a pound
From a farthing in the ground.

Money may become a curse:
Give me then my Shepherd's Purse.

~ The Song of ~ The Daisy Fairy

Come to me and play with me,
  I'm the babies' flower;
Make a necklace gay with me,
Spend the whole long day with me,
  Till the sunset hour.

I must say Good-night, you know,
  Till tomorrow's playtime;
Close my petals tight, you know,
Shut the red and white, you know,
  Sleeping till the daytime.

The Daisy Fairy

The Dandelion Fairy

The Daffodil Fairy

The Daffodil Fairy

~ THE SONG of ~
THE DOG~VIOLET FAIRY

The Dog~Violet Fairy.

The wren and robin hop around;
　　The Primrose-maids my neighbours be;
The sun has warmed the mossy ground;
Where Spring has come, I too am found:
　　The Cuckoo's call has wakened me!

~ The Song of ~
The Celandine Fairy

The
Celandine
Fairy.

Before the hawthorn leaves unfold,
Or buttercups put forth their gold,
By every sunny footpath shine
The stars of Lesser Celandine.

The Primrose Fairy.

The Primrose Fairy

~ The Song of ~
The Primrose Fairy

The Primrose opens wide in spring;
    Her scent is sweet and good:
It smells of every happy thing
    In sunny lane and wood.
I have not half the skill to sing
    And praise her as I should.

She's dear to folk throughout the land;
    In her is nothing mean:
She freely spreads on every hand
    Her petals pale and clean.
And though she's neither proud nor grand,
    She is the Country Queen.

~ The Song of ~
The Larch Fairy

Sing a song of Larch trees
    Loved by fairy-folk;
Dark stands the pinewood,
    Bare stands the oak,
But the Larch is dressed and trimmed
    Fit for fairy-folk!

Sing a song of Larch trees,
    Sprays that swing aloft,
Pink tufts, and tassels
    Grass-green and soft:
All to please the little elves
    Singing songs aloft!

The Larch
Fairy.

The Larch Fairy

The Bluebell
Fairy.

The Bluebell Fairy

~ The Song of ~ The Bluebell Fairy

My hundred thousand bells of blue,
   The splendour of the Spring,
They carpet all the woods anew
With royalty of sapphire hue;
The Primrose is the Queen, 'tis true.
     But surely I am King!
       Ah yes,
     The peerless Woodland King!

Loud, loud the thrushes sing their song;
   The bluebell woods are wide;
My stems are tall and straight and strong;
From ugly streets the children throng,
They gather armfuls, great and long,
     Then home they troop in pride—
       Ah yes,
     With laughter and with pride!

(This is the Wild Hyacinth.
The Bluebell of Scotland is the Harebell.)

~ THE SONG of ~ THE WOOD~SORREL FAIRY

The Wood Sorrel Fairy.

In the wood the trees are tall,
    Up and up they tower;
You and I are very small—
    Fairy-child and flower.

Bracken stalks are shooting high,
    Far and far above us;
We are little, you and I,
    But the fairies love us.

~ The Song of ~ The May Fairy

The
May
Fairy.

My buds, they cluster small and green;
    The sunshine gaineth heat:
Soon shall the hawthorn tree be clothed
    As with a snowy sheet.

O magic sight, the hedge is white,
    My scent is very sweet;
And lo, where I am come indeed,
    The Spring and Summer meet.

~ The Song of ~
The Speedwell Fairy

Clear blue are the skies;
   My petals are blue;
   As beautiful, too,
As bluest of eyes.

The heavens are high:
   By the field-path I grow
   Where wayfarers go,
And 'Good speed,' say I;

'See, here is a prize
   Of wonderful worth:
   A weed of the earth,
As blue as the skies!'

(There are many kinds of Speedwell:
this is the Germander.)

The Speedwell
Fairy

The Speedwell Fairy

The
Lords~and~Ladies
Fairy.

The Lords~and~Ladies Fairy

70

~ The Song of ~
The Lords-and-Ladies Fairy

Here's the song of Lords-and-Ladies
    (in the damp and shade he grows):
I have neither bells nor petals,
    like the foxglove or the rose.
Through the length and breadth of England,
    many flowers you may see—
Petals, bells, and cups in plenty—
    but there's no one else like me.

In the hot-house dwells my kinsman,
    Arum-lily, white and fine;
I am not so tall and stately,
    but the quaintest hood is mine;
And my glossy leaves are handsome;
    I've a spike to make you stare;
And my berries are a glory in September.
    (BUT BEWARE!)

(The Wild Arum has other names besides Lords-and-Ladies,
such as Cuckoo-Pint and Jack-in-the-Pulpit.)

~ The Song of ~ The Cowslip Fairy

The land is full of happy birds
And flocks of sheep and grazing herds.

I hear the songs of larks that fly
Above me in the breezy sky.

I hear the little lambkins bleat;
My honey-scent is rich and sweet.

Beneath the sun I dance and play
In April and in merry May.

The grass is green as green can be;
The children shout at sight of me.

The Cowslip Fairy.

The Cowslip Fairy

The Heart'sease Fairy.

The Heart's~Ease Fairy

~ The Song of ~
The Heart's-Ease Fairy

Like the richest velvet
    (I've heard the fairies tell)
Grow the handsome pansies
    within the garden wall;
When you praise their beauty,
    remember me as well—
Think of little Heart's-Ease,
    the brother of them all!

Come away and seek me
    when the year is young,
Through the open ploughlands
    beyond the garden wall;
Many names are pretty
    and many songs are sung:
Mine—because I'm Heart's-Ease—
    are prettiest of all!

(An old lady says that when she was a little girl the children's
name for the Heart's-Ease or Wild Pansy was
Jump-up-and-kiss-me!)

~ The Song of ~
The Lady's~Smock Fairy

Where the grass is damp and green,
Where the shallow streams are flowing,
Where the cowslip buds are showing,
    I am seen.

Dainty as a fairy's frock,
White or mauve, of elfin sewing,
'Tis the meadow-maiden growing—
    Lady's-smock.

The Lady's-Smock Fairy